BEFORE
YOU CAME
THIS WAY

BEFORE
YOU CAME
THIS WAY

by Byrd Baylor

illustrated by Tom Bahti

E. P. Dutton & Co., Inc. New York

7989

Printed in the U.S.A. by Halliday Lithograph Corporation
Published simultaneously in Canada by
Clarke, Irwin & Company Limited, Toronto and Vancouver
Library of Congress Catalog Card Number: 74-81709
SBN 0-525-26312-8
10   9   8

To the ancient unknown artists
whose drawings on stone
inspired this book.

You walk
down this canyon,
this place of
high red cliffs
and turning winds
and hawks that float
in a far white sky
and
you wonder:
"Am I the first one
ever
to come this way?"

And
you wonder:
"Is my footprint
the first one
ever
to touch this sand?"

But
then you see something
which tells you,
No,
you're not the first.
Your brothers
out of some
long ago lost age
passed this way too.

You see their marks
on canyon walls.
Even the print
of their hands
is left,
chipped deep
in stone.

These men who came before you—
    cliff dwellers,
    hunters,
    wanderers—
    left messages
    on rocks,
    on cliff sides,
    on steep rough
    canyon walls.

They drew
the things
they did
and saw.
They even drew
their corn plants

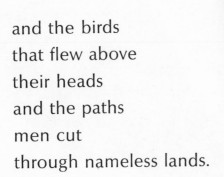

and the birds
that flew above
their heads
and the paths
men cut
through nameless lands.

The reds
and yellows
and blacks
have been battered
by a thousand winds,
washed by a thousand rains.

The pictures are dim now,
half shadow,
but you search the canyon
for them.

And here
you see
young hunters
leap
in the morning sun.
The light still
gleams on their
arrows.

And here
a coyote
howls at the moon.
From his own hill
he guards his world.
He keeps the moon
in sight.

And rabbits flick
their ears
listening

listening

listening

while men do battle.
That fierce battle
raged
loud as thunder
across this canyon
once.

You find deer
with great antlers
branching like trees.

What is it they hear?

In the wind
there's the scent
of a mountain lion
who twitches his whiskers,
twitches his tail,
as he smiles
at himself...
or the deer.

Mountain goats
with curly horns.
Goats.
Goats.
More goats.
They drew them everywhere.
The clink of sharp hoofs
must have rung
as those goats jumped
from rock
to rock
to rock—

and then jumped back where they had been before.

Two men
chased
a wild
bird
once.
And what a chase!
Now they
ALMOST
have their bird.
Not *quite*.
Not ever *quite*.

And
two animals
found
one man.
SKUNKS!
Now that man keeps
a startled look
forever
on his face.

High on a rock
someone drew
tracks of all the birds
he'd ever seen
and deer tracks,
lion tracks,
fox tracks...
even a wandering path
of the tracks of
men.

Men going where?
Searching for a
better place
for the tribe
to make its home?
Or for some newer
hunting ground?

Did pictures bring
strength
to the hunters?
Did they bring luck?
Was there some
magic
in the artist's hand?

There must have been magic
in songs and dances too...
Songs to protect
hunters,
songs to make
children grow
and corn grow
and pumpkins.

People danced.

You ALMOST know
how it must have been.

Long lines of dancers
move
into the shadows.

You ALMOST hear
the chanting
and the flute
and the rattles
and the drums
that called down rain
and made the night winds
blow.

Sometimes
the dancers put on
masks.
Their artists drew
those great fierce faces
with headdresses
so tall and bright
and feathery
that they looked
part bird,
part sky,
part mountain—
no longer men at all.

And
this canyon
echoed
with their voices.

Did they ever
wonder
who
in some far later time
would stand
in their
canyon
and think of them
and ALMOST hear
the echo of those voices
still in the wind?

A note about the illustrations

In all parts of the world we still find paintings
and drawings on rock left by early man. The illustrations
in this book are based on prehistoric Indian rock drawings
found in southwestern United States—Arizona,
New Mexico, and west Texas.

For his illustrations, Tom Bahti has used *amatl* paper,
a rough, handmade bark paper made by the Otomi Indians
of Puebla, Mexico. The art of making this paper was
known to the Indians of Mexico long before Columbus
discovered America.